MORE MYSTERY BY KRISTINE KATHRYN RUSCH

THE RETRIEVAL ARTIST SERIES

I0742572

THE SMOKEY DALTON SERIES

WRITING AS KRIS NELSCOTT

A Dangerous Road

Smoke-Filled Rooms

Thin Walls

Stone Cribs

War at Home

Days of Rage

Street Justice

WRITING AS KRIS NELSCOTT

Protectors

ALSO BY KRISTINE KATHRYN RUSCH

OR PERISH

A RUSCH CRIME STORY

KRISTINE KATHRYN RUSCH

PUBLISHING

Or Perish

Copyright © 2025 by Kristine Kathryn Rusch

Published by WMG Publishing

Cover and layout © copyright 2025 by WMG Publishing

Cover design by WMG Publishing

Cover art © copyright Canva

OR PERISH

OR PERISH

The guidelines were annoyingly obtuse.

Assistant Professor Eloise Granada sat at her desk in the corner of her shared office, near the radiator that was currently pumping out too much heat. Still, she kept a sweater on the back of her chair, because in an hour or two, the radiator would be cold and the office even colder.

Whoever decided that a radiator belonged underneath a bank of windows hadn't been thinking clearly.

At least she had learned (the hard way) not to use the wooden shelf one of her predecessors had built over the radiator. She'd ruined two different books, placing them on that shelf—one because of rain pouring in the window, and the other from the humidity coming from the radiator itself.

Her most precious books were now stored at home, but the books she needed to impress her students, colleagues, and (if she was being honest) herself were on the shelves behind her. She had built those shelves, replacing the one that covered the outdoor wall. The shelves took the triangle that was her portion of the office and made it into a cozy little nook—on the right days, anyway.

This was not one of the right days.

There was nothing cozy about this little section of not-big-enough room. At least her colleagues weren't here. They were either teaching or schmoozing. They were good at schmoozing, terrible at teaching.

Which was the opposite of her. She loved to teach.

Too bad this damn school didn't value that very much.

Gone were the days when a professor could just revel in their sinecure. Her father had done that; once he was hired at a place, he had a job unless he screwed up.

And that was *before* he had gotten tenure.

Tenure was so far in the future for Eloise—if it ever was going to happen at all—that she considered it like landing on the moon. Something a select few managed a long, long, looooooong time ago, but not something that would ever be available to her.

But she needed to make some decisions. Everyone had just gotten The Dreaded Email. The Dreaded Email arrived every January like clockwork, right after the holiday season ended but before the next term began.

The Dreaded Email was full of "you musts" and "you

shoulds," but at its core, The Dreaded Email contained the annual threat:

As we informed you in the Fall, the budget for assistant professors remains the same as it did in the last biennium. Each department will maintain its existing number of assistants throughout the calendar year....

And this part:

...in our quest to constantly improve our standing in the ranks of universities nationwide, we must evaluate each faculty member. Assistants should bring a wide variety of skills to their department, including a knowledge of the latest innovations in their field and a willingness to improve their own standing...

And then the scary part, the part they seemed to think assistant professors would forget:

Evaluations will begin in earnest in March. Qualified assistants will receive news of their status by April 30. Be sure that your curriculum vitae is up to date. Include a separate page of recent publications, honors, grants, and research projects.

And not, as she once bitched at a colleague who was no longer employed here—a colleague who was a hell of a teacher and a terrible researcher—word one about excellent student evaluations or successful and engaged classrooms.

Just publications, research, grants, and honors.

Crap that can be measured, her colleague had said, but Eloise had always begged to differ. It was possible to measure success as a teacher. It just wasn't as easy as judging the amount of someone's grant.

Knowing that—believing that to her core—did not make reading The Dreaded Email any easier. All it did was reinforce that she needed to get the hell out of here, and she wasn't sure how to do it.

Assistant professors were a dime a dozen, or maybe even a penny a dozen, given all the degrees handed out every year by the nearly 3000 colleges and universities around the United States.

She knew that number because she looked that up too, trying to figure out how to get out of here.

But getting out would be a lot easier if she was promoted to associate professor. Not only would she be one of maybe a-quarter-a-dozen associate professors in the U.S., she would also get a bump in salary, maybe big enough to enable her to save some money so that she could move somewhere—anywhere but here.

Here was once Spring Valley State Teachers College, founded in 1861. Apparently, there weren't enough teachers to come west (although by today's standards, this wasn't west at all but *Mid*west), so Spring Valley (one of a million of those too in the world) decided to lure them with a college and then force them to work one-room schoolhouses in the small and uncomfortable places for ten years before they could move to somewhere a little nicer.

Apparently, Spring Valley State Teachers College became flush with success and became a regular college seventy years later. Then, flush with all the money that colleges got from the post-World War II education boom, it started to build itself into a university.

It still had a long way to go, but that was one reason The Dreaded Email was so stringent.

This university still needed accreditation in many of its graduate programs, although not in her department. The history department.

Which was filled with bloodthirsty anxious assistants and associates who knew that they had a nearly worthless degree that could get them teaching positions in colleges and universities and almost nowhere else.

She used to say that having a nearly worthless degree in a field increasingly disrespected in a culture of now-now-now didn't bother her, but on the day she received The Dreaded Email, her degree—and her vulnerability—terrified the hell out of her.

And that was the only reason she had her computer open to the faculty tenure and promotion guidelines page. She had the damn thing memorized and knew that it hadn't really been updated in this century.

But she kept hoping for change.

Apparently, hoping for change had become her defining attribute.

Although, fortunately for her friends and her stolid and somewhat dull boyfriend, Derrick, she didn't discuss her hope-for-change attitude.

These days, she hardly discussed her work at all.

The heat from the radiator had become unbearable.

There was no way to shut the damn thing off, since someone had broken the shut-off valve before she got her precious desk here, and no matter how many times she contacted the physical plant about fixing it, maintenance had more pressing issues to deal with.

And of course, her office mates were uninterested in improving the working conditions here. For them, the radiator didn't pump out enough heat, since it seemed to gather in this corner, and do its very best to suffocate her.

That thought made her realize how much she was sweating—and that wasn't being caused by the stupid guidelines or The Dreaded Email. She was dying in here.

She shut down her office computer, leaned over, and grabbed her carryall. She unzipped it, made sure that her laptop was inside, and zipped it up again.

No papers to grade yet—not that she got them in paper anymore, because all papers had to be submitted online so that they could go through the very expensive plagiarism program that the university attached to everything. No books to carry right now either, although she had two tucked inside of it. One of those books was a thick research tome from the 1990s, and it looked as daunting as it sounded; the other book was a novel that she really didn't have time to read, but she read anyway.

What she needed was the laptop. She probably should take the books out, but that was another promise to herself: If she carried the novel, she carried the research book as well.

She wasn't really convincing anyone that she was serious about the work she was doing—anyone except herself.

And right now, her focus had to be where she stood in the Assistant Professor Sweepstakes, so she knew what she needed to do for the next two months to increase her chances.

She stood up and bumped into the wobbly credenza that the previous owner of this desk had attached. The credenza wobbled more than usual, and two books toppled off it, slamming into her right hand.

She cursed. Those damn books were heavy.

And of course, they were the last two volumes in her father's magnum opus, the thing that both made and ruined his reputation—a nine-volume history of the Republican Party from founding to the Reagan years. Volume nine, which had landed face down and open on the dirty tile floor, had been published after his death, which was lucky, considering the book's reception.

Which was a few polite reviews in the right journals and some snide commentary from people on both sides of the aisle, arguing with Dad's political opinions—the things he had strived his entire life to keep out of his work.

As he told his daughters, he had only worked in facts, and facts—in his mind—were never subject to inter-pretation.

Oh, how he would have hated the 2020s, where facts

were negotiable, and misinformation was the art form of the day.

She grabbed the book, wiped off the thin paper his publisher had given this final (massive) volume, and set it back on the wobbly credenza. Then she grabbed volume eight, which had also tried to break the fine bones in her hand, and placed it on the credenza, too.

She stared at those books. They, more than his daughters, had been his father's baby. His life's work. The be-all and end-all for his entire existence.

She kept the books as a cautionary tale for herself, that sometimes history could overtake the present and keep someone from actually living their life.

She believed that had happened to her father, and she had been determined that it wouldn't happen to her.

But she wasn't really living much of a life either. And she didn't have a wife to cater to her every need or kids who looked up to her and saw her as some kind of academic role model—even when she wasn't.

She slithered around her desk and headed into the main part of the office, noting that the temperature here was at least ten degrees cooler than it was in her little corner.

The nearest desk, belonging to Daisy Sue Mortimer, an assistant professor from the Deep South, with a specialty in the history of the Deep South (with a now-sadly trendy focus on white people), was so tidy that the desk's ancient mahogany surface literally gleamed. Instead of books on the shelf behind her desk, she kept cleaning supplies and ephoto frames of her favorite (and much missed) southern venues.

The only other personalization was a pink scarf, hanging off a peg on the side of the bookshelf. The area had a faint odor of her perfume. Eloise had no idea what it was, but she knew that most of the scent was from lilies, which she had always associated with death.

Maybe that was what Daisy Sue Mortimer represented —the death of the kind of history that Eloise valued, maybe even the death of all scholarship forever and ever.

Eloise had no idea how someone like Daisy Sue, whose first book was not published academically, but through some big-name mainstream publisher, had even gotten a job here, given the nasty faculty guidelines.

It probably had to do with her cascade of blond hair, her guileless blue eyes, and her porcelain skin. All of that looked good in the videos that seem to accompany every single "important" podcast these days.

Podcasts hadn't existed at the turn of this century as any kind of entertainment force, so they weren't mentioned in the faculty guidelines, although Eloise heard talk that they might be shoe-horned into the "or equivalent" category.

Only the academic review committee could determine if something qualified for the "or equivalent" category— and even then, they could be overruled by the academic hiring committee for a particular school (like hers, Social Science) and that academic hiring committee could be overruled by the university's hiring committee which had to review all renewals and new hires.

It was a byzantine and baroque system, designed to keep a small academic oligarchy in power. The only people who seemed to get added to that oligarchy somehow brown-nosed their way in.

It was a terrible system, one that rewarded mediocrity and the school's history, not merit, despite what the guidelines said.

Besides, that academic oligarchy had a habit of forcing the more successful professors out.

Of course, those successful professors actually had a choice of other universities to go to, although she had heard that a number of those professors were grilled about the fact that they had gotten their start at such a low-ranked university.

She had no idea what the success rate for history professors was or would be, because very few had left here. Most were part of the oligarchy, which probably shouldn't have surprised her. History was almost always a study of the people in power and how they clung to that power; it was little wonder that the scholars who specialized in that did the same thing.

She shifted her carryall to her right hand and headed toward the coat tree near the door. Doing so made her pass the final desk, which belonged to her colleague, Joseph Campbell Wanamaker. She believed, but didn't see the point of proving, that Wanamaker's name was entirely made up.

His specialty was the history of the United States as told by various big businesses—also a trendy topic, although his focus on department stores wasn't as trendy as it could have been.

Still, that—and his chiseled-jaw good looks—got him on every single so-called history program on cable television, at least the history programs that dealt with the histories of shopping and American-made companies.

Wanamaker could give a good soundbite, but he had yet to prove that he could make a "significant contribution to the overall body of scholarship in his discipline" as the faculty guidelines demanded.

And, she knew, the fact that he was good-looking in a Clark Kent sort of way—if, of course, Clark Kent's skin had been pale brown instead of pale white—counted against him. The academic oligarchy believed that the professors of this university should be pale and pasty, a little doughy, and as near-sighted as possible.

Unfortunately...or maybe fortunately...Eloise did fit into the pale, pasty, doughy, and near-sighted category.

She grabbed her sensible cloth coat off the coat tree, and pushed the door open, stepping into the hallway.

The temperature here was at least thirty degrees cooler than her little corner office, and she immediately shivered. She was not going to last through the subzero blast that would take her to faculty dining. But her stomach was beginning to growl, and she didn't have a lot of money in her account.

She had already promised herself that the Starbucks two blocks from this part of campus would be off-limits until next payday. Which was the secondary reason she was heading to faculty dining. There, she could eat for free (one of the few perks an assistant got), and the place actually had a decent selection of specialty coffees.

She moved away from her office door—from all the doors, since four opened up off this part of the hallway alone—and set her carryall down. Then she shrugged on her coat, thought for a moment about stealing Daisy Sue's scarf, and then realized that the perfume smell alone would not only give the theft away but might actually kill her.

She headed across the little reception area, where she was told that once upon a time, an actual receptionist sat. Now, the departmental assistant had a much better office than Eloise would ever get, even if she got tenure.

Departmental assistants were locked in and usually had positions that lasted forty to fifty years. Because departmental assistants weren't subject to the damn faculty guidelines.

Departmental assistants were considered non-academic employees of the university and as such were subject to state and federal employment law in a way that academics in their first few years were not.

Come to think of it, it was probably good that no departmental assistant sat at the plant-covered desk at the side of the room. Given the mood Eloise was in, she would be grumping loudly at the assistant just for existing—which really was not the assistant's fault at all.

In fact, no one sat in the reception area, because the term hadn't started yet. By the middle of the term, three or four students would be waiting nervously on the red-and-brown couch, laptop clutched nervously along their thighs. Or someone would be sitting in the black chairs near the back, gigantic headphones plastered to their ears, the music on so loud that it was possible to hear all the way down the hall.

The door to the stairwell was propped open, so someone else had been on this floor earlier. The door was supposed to be closed, but it was so damn heavy that anyone who came up here left it open so that they wouldn't have to fight it to leave.

There was an elevator on the other side of the floor, but the elevator was so slow that she could take the stairs four times before the elevator reached the ground floor.

She started into the stairwell when someone shouted from below. Eloise stopped and grabbed her phone from the side pocket of her carryall. She had learned after two years of being in the middle of a university that students could be unpredictable, and it was better to have a defense in hand. A waved phone and a threatened, *I'll call security,* usually did the trick.

There was a sound of feet scuffling on the stairs. Eloise's heart rose into her throat. Dammit. She didn't want to get in the middle of anything, but she wasn't the kind of person who could ignore a problem.

Especially a problem that could devolve into something even more serious.

"Seriously?" a vaguely familiar female said. "Twenty percent? *Twenty percent?* How in the ever-living *hell* could an entire scholarly book only count for twenty percent of my publications for the year? Are you *kidding* me?"

Uh-oh. Someone else had gotten The Dreaded Email and had probably taken their very first look at the faculty guidelines.

A male voice mumbled something that sounded placating, even from this distance.

"You're telling me," the woman said, speaking even louder, "that the nonfiction book I slaved over, that I spent *years* researching, and that got *critical acclaim* counts less than *two* articles in some lame-ass scholarly journal that has maybe five readers, four of whom were published in the same *freakin'* issue? Who the hell thought up that stupid rule?"

The academic oligarchy, Eloise wanted to say, but she didn't. Because she didn't want to go down those stairs and get into that argument. It sounded pretty heated, and she might take the wrong position with the wrong person.

Eloise had felt the same fury when she learned that real books counted less than publications in academic journals. Not that she could do anything about it.

Rules were rules, as her mother used to say.

Her father would have been furious as well. But her father had had options—not that he had ever suffered from this particular indignity. At the prestigious universities where he had worked throughout his career, the book always counted for more. The scholarly journal publications were stop-gaps for the people who needed to take a year or two or five to write their nonfiction work.

Her father had always thrown off articles like the literary dandruff they were. He published them to keep his department happy, yes, but also to keep himself in the conversation.

Not that he was in the conversation toward the end. He had made the mistake of writing a book that, in historical circles, seemed topical when her father claimed it really wasn't.

He did get approached by the political journals and major newspapers because they believed he could give them "context" on current affairs, but he reminded them all that his job was not about context. It was about the march of history.

His response had always been as strident as the woman on the stairs, which meant that no one really wanted to book him for a show or an interview because they really didn't want to spend any time with him at all.

"You tell me what I'm supposed to do now," the woman said. "You tell me. Because I wrote this thing, it's getting great acclaim—"

"From the wrong places," the man said. This time, his voice cut clearly.

"The *wrong* places? *The New York Times?* Every single book journal in the country? I've been on *Good Morning, America* and all of the cable news channels from *both* sides of the aisle, and one channel is talking about making me a regular contributor—"

"Which is nice," the man said in that dismissive tone that made Eloise's skin crawl. "But none of those are academic sources, are they?"

"Excuse me?" the woman said.

"You wrote a popular history that I'm sure will resonate clearly with the masses, but it isn't something scholarly, now is it? You have to realize that most people wouldn't know real history if it bit them in the ass so anything that sounds sensible would seem cogent to them."

Eloise let out a breath and shook her head. How many discussions had she been in like that? And those had been when she was tossing ideas around for her own book.

Hell, when she had searched for a topic for her master's thesis, her own father had said something similar.

You have to decide if you're going to be a scholar or if you're going to be a popular historian. Or a historical novelist. If you want to teach, then you'll need to be a scholar.

She shook his voice out of her head, shoved her phone in the right pocket of her coat, and backed away from the stairwell. She wasn't going to get involved in that mess.

She thought of going to the elevator, but she knew that

would be futile. Instead, she headed back the way she came and walked to the Political Science Department. There was a stairwell over there.

Usually, the Poli Sci Department was empty. Those professors did spend a lot of time on mostly local media, talking about current events.

On this day, though, several of her colleagues in the Assistant Professor Sweepstakes were clustered together, speaking in low tones.

She had done that too the very first time she had received The Dreaded Email and read, really read, the faculty guidelines. She'd talked about fighting it, about seeing the then newly minted president of the university, of bringing the matter to the media and talking on TV about the grievances…when an older assistant had said, in measured and somewhat sad tones, *They don't understand why this is bad. They think we're whining.*

She had gotten that from Derrick, who had told her to write the book she wanted to write, this bogus scholarship thing be damned.

The cluster of assistants focused on Anastasia Lundgren. She was a tall woman, who lived just outside of town on a farm. She offered to bring in cords of wood to anyone with a wood-burning fireplace and always reminded people that she cut the wood herself.

Stress relief, she would say, although it seemed like a colossal waste of time to Eloise.

"Maybe I'm horribly optimistic," Anastasia was saying,

"but it seems to me that at some point, they're going to have to make changes. They can't sustain a university without assistants and associates. Besides, they pay us less than the full professors and heads of the department. We're saving them money."

That was a full 180 from her position last year. Last year, on her first Dreaded Email Day, Anastasia was one of the loudest, complaining that the rules designed in the 1970s should remain in the 1970s.

She seemed amazingly calm this year. Either she had another job offer or someone had told her that she was going to get promoted based on her somewhat shaky scholarship.

"We've been saying that for years," Colin Overmyer said, "and nothing has changed."

Micah Amiri started to shake his head, and then his gaze landed on Eloise. He smiled. He always greeted her with that kind of warmth, and it always unnerved her a little.

She wasn't used to handsome men smiling at her. And he was handsome. He was a dark-haired, dark-eyed man, who was just a little too slender. His specialty was the Persian Gulf region, so he was always in demand. His parents had fled Iran after the fall of the Shah, and he had a lot of familial experience to draw on.

She'd actually read his doctoral thesis before he had turned it in, and it was brilliant. But he was young and new. The larger schools had people with longer pedigrees who had been writing about that region for decades, some of them actual scholarly refugees, and therefore had no need of someone like him.

This department had thoughts of grooming him into one of their prestige professors, but that would take years —and some strategic scholarship on his part.

"Eloise," he said. "You've been through this. Help us—"

"Can't!" she said as cheerfully as she could. "I have a can't-miss meeting."

With some kind of sugary coffee drink and maybe lunch. But she didn't add that part.

Instead, she waved her free hand in a kind of dismissal and stepped into the stairwell. It was narrower than the history department's favorite stairwell and not as clean. There were cobwebs in the upper corners of the landings. Apparently, most everyone in the Poli Sci department took the elevators, and no one had flagged the cleaning of the stairwell for the janitorial staff.

She hurried down, her feet clanging on the metal stairs. She purposely made a lot of noise, so that if someone thought of arguing in the stairwell, they could save it until she was gone.

But she saw no one.

She reached the bottom and found herself faced with a narrow door that was giving off a lot of chill. She had forgotten that this door opened into a side alley behind the building—which was probably another reason no one ever took it.

She shoved the door open, and it scraped on some ice. No one had come this way in a long time.

Still, she persisted, not wanting to go up a floor and wend her way through other departments, probably filled with worried assistant professors.

She had to shove hard. The door caught on even more ice, and the ice was—oddly—pink. She looked down, and saw an ungloved hand. It was slightly blue, and it was attached to a wrist, and that wrist was wearing a watch.

Someone had fallen on the ice, and she hoped to God that they hadn't already frozen to death.

She stepped back inside the stairwell for just a moment because if she went outside, the door would close behind her, and would be locked. She wouldn't be able to get back in.

It was against regulations all over the university to prop open doors, but there was always a rock or a brick or something that would keep one of these doors from closing.

Except here, of course. She couldn't see any rock or brick or even one of the practical metal doorstops that existed in some of the newer buildings.

So, she set down her carryall, reached inside, removed the thick research book, and propped it between the door and its frame. If that book got destroyed, so be it. It had 8-point type and was dry as dust anyway.

Then she made sure the book was in the right position

so that she couldn't accidentally knock it loose and lock herself out.

She became methodical in a crisis, something her father and her sisters hated about her. But they also used it, particularly in the crisis years after her mother died unexpectedly.

That Eloise—the practical, methodical, and emotionally cold one—was the one who stepped outside of the door. She knew to avoid the pink ice and to take a wide step to the snow beyond it.

This part of the quad was empty, not that she was really in the quad at all. She was in a slight alcove formed by the buildings, with a small concrete wall between them that held some kind of equipment maintained by the physical plant.

She turned, so she could see the extent of the problem, and gasped.

A man in shirt sleeves lay on his side, his face facing the building. She had shoved him slightly backwards when she had pushed on the door—if the position of the door and his body was any indication.

He was wearing shirt sleeves. A sweater was tied around his waist and bunched up against his back, again, probably from the way that she had shoved him backwards.

Blood was pooled around his head. A lot of blood, some of which had seeped into the snow. The top layer of blood, though, was black, which meant that it had coagulated.

He must have come out, figured he could get back in, slipped and hit his head.

Although he was lying on his side, not his back.

And the back of his head was bashed in. No, caved in. No…not really there at all.

That made her start to shake. She called on her calm, rational self because if she panicked, this entire situation would get much, much worse.

She pulled the phone out of her pocket and used voice activation rather than try to dial 911 with her mittens on.

Someone answered quickly and asked her what her emergency was.

She told them that she had found someone lying in the snow.

"I think he hit his head," she said, being deliberately naïve because she wasn't a doctor or a first responder or a police officer. She wasn't going to be saying the guy was dead, because she didn't want to touch him to confirm it.

The dispatch asked her to describe where she was and what she was seeing, and asked her to stay on the line until the paramedics arrived.

She promised she would, and resisted the urge to ask if she should give the poor man her coat. Because, as nice as the offer would have been, it would have been fruitless, given what else she could see.

What she could see were his eyes, wide open and blank, staring at the door in front of him as if it had mesmerized him while he died slowly, unable to get inside the building or call anyone for help.

The paramedics arrived four minutes later. Her phone thoughtfully provided the length of the call, which told her the arrival time. She hung up on the dispatch and shoved the phone in her pocket, knowing that the EMTs might've gotten here sooner if they hadn't had to bring an ambulance with them.

The brand-new university hospital building was just across the quad, the other direction from the faculty dining room where she should have been at this very minute. Walking was easier to get to those parts of campus. Driving meant twisty service lanes or big roads with too many stop signs.

She was a bit amazed the EMTs had made it as quickly as they had.

They parked haphazardly, tailgate toward the buildings, and one of the EMTs got out, while the other opened the back of the ambulance.

The one who had gotten out started to sprint toward her, and then stopped as he realized just how icy the ground was. He walked toward her, stepping carefully with his big black boots.

He was carrying some kind of emergency kit in his ungloved hands. He wore a winter jacket over his stupidly white official shirt, and his pants were tucked into those boots.

He looked younger than she was, which made her feel nervous. She wanted someone with a lot of experience, given what was going on right now.

As the EMT got closer, she realized she was in his way. She stepped backwards, into deeper snow, and felt some of it slide into her short boots. Great. Now her feet were going to get wet.

She was already cold.

But as she moved, she realized she had been standing stock still ever since she left the building.

The EMT didn't ask her if this was the guy, because it obviously was the guy. Instead, the EMT slipped on some blue medical gloves he'd had in his pocket and knelt beside the man.

He touched the skin lightly and was going to shine a light in the man's eyes but stopped when he saw that they were already glazed over.

Eloise watched all of this with a detachment that surprised her. She had been good in all the familial emergencies, but this emergency was weird and sad and made her deeply uncomfortable in a way she would unpack later.

Finally, the EMT rocked back on his heels. He said to her, "I'm sorry, ma'am, but he's dead."

The sentence was delivered compassionately yet impersonally because the paramedic had no tie to this man, maybe even to the university, and certainly no tie to Eloise.

Then the EMT moved his other hand in a kind of wave, directed at the second EMT who had been watching from the back of the ambulance. That EMT nodded—apparently message received—and then closed the back doors.

They wouldn't be transporting someone to a hospital. They were going to have to wait with the body until the police arrived.

She took a deep breath, wanting to ask if she could leave, which part of her thought was callous and part of her thought of as pure survival.

She didn't ask it, though, because she knew what the answer would be.

Instead, she stood in the snow, listening to the EMT use some kind of radio code for police assistance, probably a code that told them they'd be dealing with a body.

Then the second EMT came over. He stopped near the path and crouched as if he had found another body. Instead, he removed a phone from his pocket and took a picture.

She couldn't see what he was photographing.

He stood up and came over to her.

"Ma'am," he said politely, "let's move you to the sidewalk. I'm sure the police will want to talk with you."

Even though she had done nothing, the words sent a shiver through her. If she had been the one to bash this poor guy's head in, then she would have been terrified.

But she wasn't. She was still detached.

She clutched her carryall and followed the second EMT

along the same path he had used to reach her. As she walked, she noted the one thing that had apparently caught his attention earlier.

There was pink snow maybe two yards away from the body. Pink snow, and in the middle of it, a brown brick with a broken edge.

She didn't know for sure, but she could guess where that brown brick had come from. There hadn't been one near the door. Someone had grabbed it and used it against the dead guy.

That would make it a crime of passion, something that had been unplanned and which had happened on the spur of the moment.

Somehow, that did not make her feel better.

And it didn't really make sense either. Because the dead guy was *outside*, facing the door, and whoever had killed him had been behind him.

So maybe a few other doors were also missing their bricks.

Still, she might have to tell the police about this.

Although she remembered from her Politics of Protest class, the one she had taken as an undergraduate at a public university with a proud history of protest, that one should never ever volunteer information to the police.

One should always let the police lead the questioning and then, if the questioning got a bit contentious, one should ask for a lawyer.

She hoped she wouldn't need a lawyer just because she

had stumbled on a body. She couldn't afford a lawyer, and if things got bad, she'd have to ask one of her sisters for help.

They already thought less of her because she taught here. Her sister Emma, the family's best scholar according to their father, had already received a coveted associate professorship at Yale, and her sister Evangeline was on her way to becoming one of the foremost experts in women's studies, with a career-making turn at UCLA.

Her sisters had professorial and publishing money—not a lot, but more than Eloise had.

They also had prestige, and, she would wager, they had never discovered a body turned sideways in the snow.

She studied the poor man as the second EMT returned to him. Apparently, they had systems for handling the sudden discovery of bodies, protecting the scene while doing things. That left her to stamp her soaking wet feet and wrap her arms around her inadequate cloth coat.

She should have stolen Daisy Sue's muffler after all.

At that thought, the cavalry arrived—or rather, several squad cars, all with the lights on.

She didn't realize until they arrived that she had seen no one else, even though she had heard some faint end-of-class bells.

Of course, someone had already put the university on lockdown. She had been holding her phone. Surely, she would have gotten a notification.

Then she remembered that she had put her phone in

her pocket. This cloth coat might not have been warm enough, but it was thick enough that she probably hadn't felt her phone buzz—and that's all it would have done, since she kept the sound turned off the entire time she was on campus.

The police cars surrounded the ambulance. They left the lights on, the blue and red reflecting off the snow, the road, and the white side of the building closest to her.

Two officers got out—a man and a woman—and they weren't wearing coats. Their uniforms were heavy, and their gear was on a belt attached snugly to their hips. She couldn't identify half the things they wore and wasn't even going to try.

They glanced at her, but didn't say anything as they loped toward the EMTs. One of the EMTs held up a hand —which apparently meant *stop* because both officers did.

Two other officers got out of another squad car, and one of them walked over to her. That officer wore a heavy cap over their face, hair pulled back so that only their high cheekbones and solid jawline were visible.

The officer used a bare knuckle to tilt the hat's bill back, revealing deep brown eyes with long lashes. With that jawline, Eloise hadn't been expecting a woman.

"You discovered the body?" the police officer asked.

"Yeah," Eloise said, and was about to launch into an explanation, then remembered that she shouldn't offer too much information.

"I'm going to ask you to tell me what happened," the police officer said. "I may not be the only one."

"I understand," Eloise said, and waited.

The police officer then walked her through the discovery of the body, step by step.

Eloise did her best to concentrate on her answers, but it was hard. Other police officers were hurrying by her, and a few were standing in a cluster. Some had gone to other parts of campus, while others were directing campus security, all the while keeping everyone away from an ever-expanding crime scene.

The EMTs spoke to a different officer and then returned to their ambulance—apparently to await more instructions.

Eloise had been part of a campus lockdown in high school. It had been terrifying—hiding in a classroom and being as quiet as possible. No one had gotten hurt; the lockdown, it turned out, had been because someone with a gun had threatened a staff member just outside the school zone.

She had never been completely clear on what had happened; she had simply been aware of the sheer terror of the afternoon, which was probably something the scattered people on campus were experiencing as well.

"Did you see anyone at all?" the officer asked for maybe the fifteenth time. "Anyone near here, anyone in the building who might have fled the scene?"

"No," Eloise said. "I didn't see anything until I found him. Do you know who he is?"

"His name is Angus Carlson," a male voice said from behind her. "He's a professor here."

Eloise turned ever so slightly. The owner of the voice was maybe fifty, with silver hair combed back, and craggy sunbaked skin. He had ruddy cheeks from that same sunbaking, and a nose that clearly had been broken at least once.

"Detective Richard Staggher," the man said, shoving his hands in a long cloth coat. "I caught this one."

"Eloise Granada," she said, not wanting to use her assistant professor title because it felt so small.

"What do you know about Professor Carlson?" Staggher asked.

"*Doctor* Carlson," she said reflexively. Because Carlson himself had always corrected anyone who called him "professor," saying it was a lesser title, one "anyone" could get.

Which was kinda sorta true. After all, she was a professor now, but an assistant. She had a doctorate as well —everyone on the faculty had to have one—but hers was fairly newly minted and Dr. Carlson's had been handed out in the Jurassic Period.

"*Doctor* Carlson," Staggher said with an ever-so-slight smile, as if he had caught her at something. "So you knew him."

"Everyone knew him," she said, feeling odd about the

past tense. She glanced over at the door. All she could see was Dr. Carlson's feet, and they looked oddly vulnerable.

He wasn't wearing boots. He was wearing dress shoes, which struck her as strange, because of the snow and the ice.

She seemed to recall that on non-snowy days, he wore galoshes over his shoes which he called "rubbers" and made everyone laugh. Not with him. *At* him, because he had no idea about the double meaning.

Or if he did, he didn't care.

She had always opted for the *didn't care* side of him. He seemed unable to care about anything at all except his own interests.

"It doesn't sound like you liked him," Staggher said.

She made herself focus on the detective. "I—he…" She stopped. Anything she said here was going to reflect badly on her. "It's complicated."

"Uncomplicate it for me," Staggher said. His tone, slightly supercilious and mostly serious, irritated her. It was as if he had already judged her.

"I—um—he…" There she was, saying the same thing again. "We…*we*…were from different generations."

There, that was slightly innocuous. She wasn't sure if that was good enough.

Staggher raised his eyebrows. "You found a man dead, and all you can say is that you're from different generations?"

"I'm sorry he's dead," she said, and as the words came

out of her mouth, she wondered if that was true. Then, as she thought about it, she decided it was true. Because even though she had never liked him, she hadn't hated him...enough.

She suspected one would need a great deal of hatred in order to kill another human being.

"We'll get an approximate time of death shortly," Staggher said, "but from what I'm hearing, he'd been out here a while. Where were you, say, two hours ago?"

In my office, she nearly said, *reading an email he was responsible for.*

"In my office," she said, catching the last part of the sentence so that she didn't say it. "One of my students stopped by right after I got there. He needed a letter of recommendation so that he could get into an upper-level class."

"I thought letters of recommendation were for getting into a university," Staggher said.

She smiled at him, and she knew—and she couldn't help it—that the smile was condescending.

"Universities and their rules can be exceedingly complicated," she said. "Each school is different, and each school swears by its rules."

Then she shivered, as her own words caught her. Normally, she would have said that each school lived and died by its rules. She did not say that here.

She was already editing her own thoughts.

"Do you need more from me right now?" she asked. "Because I did not expect to be out here so long."

"Where were you going when you found him?" Staggher asked.

"To get something to eat." She looked in the direction of the faculty dining room. People had started moving across the quad again. Apparently, the all-clear had gone out. No one thought a nutball with a load of bricks was running around, attempting to beat students to death.

"And you went out this door?" he asked, waving his hands at the door she had used.

"Shortcut," she said. "It's easier to go across the quad than it is to walk on the paths."

He nodded. "You gave your statement to the officer?"

"Yeah," she said.

"We'll follow up," he said.

She sighed. "I would expect nothing less."

He gave her a sad little smile, almost regretful, as if he didn't want the conversation to end, or maybe as if he had never believed her in the first place.

Then he walked past her and ducked under crime scene tape that officers were starting to post along the entire distance between the buildings.

So, there was no going back up to her office, not that she wanted to. She could either go to her car and just drive home, maybe take a warm bath when she got there, and try to calm down, or she could squelch her way to the faculty dining room.

She was still hungry, and she wondered what that said about her. She had just found a man she had known for three years dead on the sidewalk, and all she could think about was the next meal.

And changing her socks. She had some extra socks in her carryall, as well as a pair of tennis shoes she usually wore in the non-snowy months. She kept them in there even after she had realized that she wasn't required to dress up on campus, like she had had to do at her first teaching job.

Still, she stood still for a moment, confounded by the change in her university. There were police everywhere, yellow security tape going up in an area that she would normally walk through, and students staring at the procedures as if they were confused by them. Experts—she had no idea what kind except that they were wearing white Tyvek suits over their winter gear—worked on the body.

She had no idea what kind of work they were actually doing, because didn't they figure out things like the cause of death in an autopsy in a lab? She wasn't going to ask, though.

She sighed heavily and decided she couldn't take more of this, no matter how hungry she was. People in the faculty dining room would have questions. Or they'd be talking excitedly about what had happened to them during the brief lockdown.

If she went to the faculty dining room, at some point, she would have to admit that she had been the one to call

911, and then there would be questions, questions she didn't want to answer.

So, she turned away from the flashing lights and the ambulance and the crime scene tape, and squelched her way to the faculty parking garage. Her car was on the topmost level, where all the assistants parked, because there was no elevator.

Normally, she wouldn't have minded, but on this day, she minded. All the tiny little micro indignities that went with her assistant position, so different from the micro indignities that had gone with her doctoral study, and even more different from the micro-indignities that had gone with her master's.

Of course she was thinking about those as she walked across the icy road to the six-story parking structure. Of course she was.

Because most of the micro-indignities she suffered on this campus had come from Dr. Carlson and his colleagues.

She lied about not having an opinion of them.

She hated them all.

The housing she had gotten through the university by waiting in the two longest lines of her life was barely adequate. It wasn't even a house, really, more like a row house, although no one called it that.

Thank heavens she shared walls on both sides, because

in a cold like this, she would have suffered a lot more if she hadn't gotten residual heat from her neighbors.

The front door stuck, and the back door barely latched, so she didn't use that. Instead, she parked out front and used the front walk, which, unlike her neighbors, she kept shoveled.

The neighborhood was dim in the afternoon light, even though there had been sunlight earlier. She unlocked her door and pushed on it. For once, it didn't stick, and she stumbled inside.

The interior was toasty, which meant her neighbors had their heat on full. She didn't mind. She set down her carryall, removed her coat and put it in the narrow coat closet—and, maybe for the first time since she moved here —she doublechecked that the front door was locked.

It was. She pulled the curtains closed, then toed off her boots. She put one hand on the wall between the window and the door. The wall was ice-cold, which wasn't a surprise. She yanked off her soaking wet socks, then left them beside the boots on the mat she kept for just this purpose.

Her feet were bright red and a little swollen, and they ached. No wonder she had gotten so very cold. Her poor feet were suffering.

She was going to have to go upstairs and run a bath, but she needed to eat first. Besides, if she stuck her feet in hot water right now, the pain would be excruciating.

She made herself walk across the uneven wood floor,

past her ancient sofa, and into the tiny kitchen. It was square and had been built in the 1950s, just like the rest of this complex. The electric stove was half the size of a modern stove, and the refrigerator was not even as tall as she was.

Still, the kitchen made the house. She had room for a tiny table, and the view of the fenced-in back yard, filled with trees, calmed her every time.

Except this time.

She had started shaking, and she didn't think that was from the cold. She was finally having a reaction. She grabbed her tea kettle, filled it, and put it on the stove. Then she set out her tea supplies and grabbed the half sandwich she had left over from a splurge at a really good off-campus sandwich shop.

She set that on the table, put her hands on the back of the stupidly comfortable caned-back chair that had come with the house, and bowed her head.

Dr. Angus Carlson. God, she hated him. He was mean, condescending, and sexist. He had never really made his way into the 21st century, leaving it to his graduate and post-doc students to handle all the "interfering technology" that the university "forced" on the professors.

His economics classes used books that had originally been published in the 1980s and were becoming increasingly difficult to get in that particular edition. His class on The Economic History of the United States ended in 2000, because he claimed (and, to be fair, Eloise's father would

37

have agreed) that anything that occurred after that was not yet settled, and still had a major impact on today's economics.

Eloise would have argued—and had, just once, in front of him (unfortunately)—that the economic history of the 1780s still had an impact on the economics of the United States. She had said that in a faculty conclave as they planned for a special historical conference. His face had turned bright red (not the blue-gray it was now), and he had screamed at her, telling her that she should never contradict him in front of *his* peers, particularly when she was a lowly *assistant* and he had decades of experience in academia.

Three months later, he was the only one on the academic hiring committee who had voted against the continuation of her contract. Last year, he had stopped her in the hall two days before the vote and asked her if she had come to her senses about economic history.

She had learned by then how important he was to university politics, so she had given him what she privately called her *dumb-girl* smile, and said, *It was my mistake, Dr. Carlson. I have since read your works, sat in on one of your classes, and given it all some thought. I was quite wrong, and I'm sorry about that.*

He had smiled at her then, revealing a gold tooth toward the back of his mouth, something she didn't think was even done anymore. Then he patted her on the shoulder, called her a good girl as if she was a pet dog, and went on his way.

After that moment, she did everything she could to avoid him, as did most assistant and associate professors. He was the roadblock to so many promotions. And he was the head of the academic oligarchy, the man who decided which new professor got to replace someone who retired or simply had had enough and resigned every single one of their committee appointments—something that had happened more than once in the short time Eloise had been connected to the university.

Her tea kettle whistled, startling her. She had been gripping the back of the chair so tightly that her fingers hurt.

She let go of the chair and shook off the pain. She shut off the burner, moved the kettle to another burner, and slid her mug forward, tea bag already inside.

Then she poured the water, steaming upwards. She leaned her face into it, feeling the moisture on her skin, warming her all the way down.

She wasn't going to cry for this man. She wasn't even sorry he was dead—and part of her thought she should be sorry he was dead. Part of her believed she should feel bad anytime anyone died.

But he was such an asshole, such a self-important jerk, that all she could feel was relief that she wouldn't have to dodge him in the halls any longer.

Her life had just gotten better because he had left the planet.

And then she paused, as a thought reached the front of her brain.

Her life had gotten better and, she suspected, so had the lives of many others as well.

She had never been around a murder before and, she just realized, the solution to this one was not going to be very simple.

Eloise didn't sleep much that night. She kept waking up in a panic, first about finding the body (did the police suspect her?), then about the continuation of her assistant professor contract (or maybe gunning for the promotion, now that Dr. Carlson was dead [and oh, that thought made her feel guilty]), and then finally, the pink snow. She kept panicking about the pink snow, wondering why she hadn't seen drops of pink leading somewhere, maybe even the door she had come out of.

Midway through the night, she was tangled in the blankets in her tiny bedroom, car lights cascading over the ceiling, waking her up, as they did every night when her neighbors came home.

But she was so panicked that at first she thought the bright white lights were from the police, coming to arrest her. That thought made her wake all the way up and focus on all of her little panicked moments.

She finally caught herself, mentally shook herself off, and got out of bed to maybe clear her head.

She realized then, as her awake brain began to ponder everything, that she hadn't seen pink drops in the snow because blood was hot. It would have carved little holes in the snow, and then, if there had been more snow or a wind, those little holes would have vanished.

It had been up to the crime scene techs in their Tyvek uniforms to figure out where, exactly, the blood trail was. It wasn't up to her.

None of it was up to her. She wouldn't be important at all going forward, except maybe if the police caught the murderer and there was a trial. Then, maybe, she would be on the witness stand—*Yes, your honor. No, your honor. I understand, your honor—just the facts. Well, I tried to open the door...*

She shook that off too, thought for a brief moment that maybe she should call one of her sisters and have them talk her down, but Emma would turn the conversation to her own accomplishments as usual, and Evangeline would wonder aloud if Eloise's treatment by the police was changed at all from the way they might have treated a man.

She didn't need anything of that.

Then, and only then, did she think of contacting Derrick. In theory, he should have been her first call when she got home that night, but he wasn't. It had taken her hours of lonely rumination in front of the television set, as well as panicked dreaming, before his name even came up.

Even now, in the middle of the night, she really didn't want to call him. She couldn't even imagine it, really. If he came over, he would want to sleep with her "to calm her down" after, of course, they discussed what she had seen.

Even then, she would have to explain all of her complex feelings, from the fear that somehow got triggered in her (*Do you think the murderer will come after someone else?*) to the fact that there was a tiny part of her (okay, a not-so-tiny part) that wanted to celebrate Dr. Carlson's untimely end.

She wasn't sure she liked the way she was reacting to Dr. Carlson's death, but she didn't dislike her (very private) emotions enough to try to change them or even share them.

She was downstairs in her tiny kitchen by the time she came to that conclusion. The sun hadn't come up yet, but it wouldn't be long before it did.

If she went back to bed now, she would get maybe another hour of sleep, and she wasn't sure if that would harm her or help her.

The day ahead was one of her shorter workdays. She could come home in the mid-afternoon, nap, and grapple with the promotion problems. She still had three months. That was plenty of time to apply for a few research grants and almost enough time to get an article in the process at one of the scholarly journals.

Too bad that the university didn't have its own reputable scholarly journal in the history department... although it did run quite a prestigious scholarly journal in economics, and, she had learned through one of her colleagues, they were always short of good *readable* material.

Good, readable material.

She didn't like how her brain was working now. Maybe she could write a fuck-you to Dr. Carlson—and no one would really know about the inspiration except her.

In less than a minute, the idea went from random thought to fully developed outline in her head. She even knew what sources she would use and how she would make the piece more marketable to various scholarly journals should the one here at the university not take it.

Because, not only was Dr. Carlson wrong about economic history, but her father had been wrong too. Her father had believed that political parties guided America to or through their various crises. In fact, his thesis on the Republican Party had been a simple one: The Republican Party had held the secret to America in the mid-to-late 19th century and had lost what it meant to be an American by the mid-to-late 20th century.

Sure, lots of scholars had argued the point *ad infinitum* as each of her father's books were published, but no one had ever argued with his premise—that political parties and the groups that formed them were the most important part of politics in America.

And yet, and yet, that was so wrong. As James Carville had said in 1992, "It's the economy, stupid!"

He was more right than not. The economy that the

Founders knew created the underpinning for the country itself. The economy that the Founders built (original oligarchs that they were) included slavery and land-ownership, as well as a small group of the wealthy who were the only people whom the Founders believed were worth governing the country.

That belief led to the creation of the Jacksonian Democrats, led to the big battles of the Civil War, led to the New Deal…

She grabbed the yellow legal pad she always kept in the junk drawer and scrawled her ideas on it until her stomach claimed that it needed sustenance to continue. She actually stopped and made herself an omelet, something she hadn't done in months.

Then she ate, wrote, and drank some tea before surfacing again, realizing that she barely had time to shower to get ready for her 9 a.m. meeting.

Her mood was almost giddy, and she tried to talk herself down in the shower. It wouldn't do, the day after she discovered a dead body, to be happier than she had been the day before.

So she tried to be somber. She wore a black sweater over grayish-black jeans and hauled some black boots out of the back of her closet, figuring her short boots wouldn't be dry yet.

She packed up the carryall, which was lighter than she expected. She had never grabbed that horrid research book. Oh, well, at least she hadn't left the novel behind.

Then she realized she hadn't even looked at her email since she discovered the body, and dithered for a moment, wondering if the pre-semester meetings had been canceled (she could only hope!). She looked on her phone, found that they hadn't been (drat!) and scrambled out the front door, nearly forgetting to lock it.

It had snowed overnight, and her black boots were barely adequate to the task of walking through two inches of the white stuff to the car. She scraped and shoved and pushed the snow off her vehicle, and promised herself that she wouldn't drive distracted although, of course, she did drive distracted—her mother's voice rising in her head: *Promise me you won't be scholarly*, her mother had said after her father's fifth time driving into something because he had been thinking about his research instead of the road in front of him.

Still, somehow between the ghosts of her parents and the whispers of excitement over her freedom to write something she actually cared about, she made it not only to the parking garage but to her office as well.

She didn't take the stairwell at any time, though—not even the nearby stairwell. She was swearing off stairwells for the foreseeable future, even if it meant spending half her life in the World's Slowest Elevator.

The departmental staff meeting had been moved to the afternoon, which disappointed her because she wanted her day to end early. The meeting had been moved because the 9 a.m. slot was being taken by the university president, who held a meeting for all staff in the Skyelr Auditorium.

The meeting was supposed to be closed, but of course, it wasn't. There was press toward the back (President Whitley loved his press), and it seemed to her that Staggher was hanging back there too, alongside someone who looked as officially unofficial as he did.

The Dean of the School of Social Sciences, Stefano Chizer, was seated on the stage with President Whitby, as was the acting chair of the Economics Department, Hayden Dillenger. They looked very uncomfortable and kept sending glances to the back of the room, as if the press —or maybe the not-so-subtle police presence—bothered them.

Eloise decided to ignore them all. She took her usual seat in the middle and listened to the updates. Yes, it had been Dr. Carlson who had been killed. Yes, the killer was still at large. No, the police did not believe there was a threat to the entire campus.

There were other details—counselors available for anyone who felt they needed it, someone else would be taking Dr. Carlson's seminars, and his committee assignments would be subject to university review.

Anyone with business pending with Dr. Carlson could talk to his assistant or with one of the other professors in the Economics department. His official functions on campus were being dealt with outside of the administrative office, so if you didn't have economics business, come to the administrative office and leave a name.

President Whitby lamented the loss, particularly at the joyous and busy time at the beginning of the semester, but he reminded everyone, it was their duty to make the incoming students feel safe and supported.

Even though there was a murderer at large. Of course, he didn't say that part. No one said that part, but a lot of people in the economics department were giving each other the side eye.

Or maybe that side eye was only because, Eloise had a hunch, the competition for department chair was going to be particularly fraught.

There was a moment of silence, notification of funeral arrangements, which the university itself was doing. Dr. Carlson had no family to speak of. (*The university was his life*, President Whitby said.) The university would designate where to send flowers and/or donations by the end of day, since Dr. Carlson (in typical form) had not designated a charity for that before his death. Eloise got the sense that Dr. Carlson, arrogant asshole that he was, hadn't even had a will despite the fact he was in his mid-seventies.

President Whitby gave the stage to Dr. Chizer, who both reassured everyone in the school of social sciences that he was up to the task of taking them through "this difficult time," and also scared the crap out of them by reminding them that Dr. Carlson's office had become part of a crime scene.

"Please give our police officers the utmost courtesy," Dr. Chizer said. "I'm told they'll be on campus for a while."

There were some actual moans about that, which Eloise thought quite strange. But the faculty didn't like its routines disturbed.

Then Dr. Chizer reminded everyone that classes will begin on Monday, despite the tragedy, and he expected everyone to be prepared.

"However," he said, "if you are having difficulties because of yesterday's events and feel that you can't commit to teaching a full semester right now, please talk with me. We will see what we can work out."

Then he nodded at the professors along the side of the stage, all of whom, Eloise realized, were chairs of their various departments.

President Whitby returned to the stage, and Eloise expected him to end the meeting right there. Instead, President Whitby gestured to the back and, after a moment, who should step onto the stage, but Staggher himself.

He didn't use platitudes, nor did he mince words. He introduced himself and said he would be present on campus for the next week or so, and anyone with information should contact him or the other detective on the case, Laurel Frazier. She was the officially unofficial person still leaning against the wall, and she waved a hand so that everyone would see her—although Eloise had the sense that Detective Frazier preferred to conduct her investigations stealthily, not with any kind of fanfare at all.

The meeting ended, and the conversation was subdued. Usually, after meetings involving the entire staff, there was complaining mixed with a lot of defense. This time, people filed out without talking at all.

Eloise didn't feel like talking either. She kept her head down and made no eye contact. All she wanted to do was get back to her office, finish the handful of tasks she had before the semester started, and get back to outlining her article.

She was even thinking it could be a book.

"Hey, Eloise!" The voice belonged to Micah.

She didn't want to talk to him. She didn't want to talk to anyone, not right now.

Still, she stopped and turned. There he was, behind her, wearing a flannel shirt over a black turtleneck that accented his eyes. He had slung his laptop bag over one shoulder.

He reached her side, bringing with him the scents of coffee and sugar. That was when she noted the gigantic Starbucks cup in his left hand.

"I hear you found him," he said, and she braced herself. She hadn't expected these questions, but of course, they were going to come at her, and they were going to come from everyone.

"Yeah," she said. "Can we walk? Because I have a lot to do today."

Micah didn't answer that. Instead, he tilted his head slightly, his gaze probing.

"Listen, I've come across bad things in the course of my life..." Then he shook his head and stopped himself. "I just wanted to ask if you were okay. Something like that, no matter who the person is, is hard."

To her surprise, tears pricked her eyes and she wasn't sure if she should blink (because the last thing she wanted was one of those tears to fall) or wipe her eyes (calling attention to her emotions) or pretend she wasn't feeling anything at all.

It was no surprise to herself that she chose the last one. That was the only way to move forward, after all.

"I'm okay," she said.

He put his free hand on her shoulder. His touch was warm.

"You're not," he said softly, "and that's okay."

If he kept this up, she really would cry.

"You might want to talk with one of those counsellors," he said.

She shook her head. "I don't need to," she said. "I'm okay."

She put a bit of emphasis on *okay*, maybe to convince herself as well as him.

That compassionate look was almost more than she could take. Then he squeezed her shoulder and nodded just a little.

"Look, I get it," he said. "Counsellors may not be your thing. In that case, I'd say my office door is always open, but I don't really have an office, so I'm happy to meet for coffee. I can be a sympathetic ear."

He wasn't Derrick, who wouldn't understand at all. He wasn't her sisters, who had their own sinecures and who would probably channel her father and say, *See what happens at half-assed universities?*

Micah had even gotten The Dreaded Email, so he knew how it all factored in.

"Yeah, okay," she said. "That...that...that would be nice. I have your number, right? I'll text you."

And then she slipped away from him, not sure what emotions were filling her. She wanted to focus on her work, not on how she felt. How she felt was irrelevant right now.

She had a lot to do.

She put her head down again and caught up to the crowd. There still wasn't much conversation, and what little there was seemed subdued. Mostly, the conversations were about who would replace Dr. Carlson on the committees.

No one seemed to have anything kind to say about the man. No one seemed to be mourning his loss. Some people, in fact, were annoyed at him for getting himself killed. The phrasing was, she thought, telling.

She reached her building and took the Slowest Elevator In The World to her floor. As she waited for the door to creak open, she thought about how many seconds she was going to waste every single time she got on this thing, just to get in or out of it.

The elevator door finally opened to reveal clusters of people staring at her. They filled the reception area, standing in small groups, and looking at her almost guiltily.

She nodded at them, almost as if she was giving them permission to finish their conversations, and then trudged to her office, noting most of the other doors in the long hallway were open.

So was her door, which never happened. She was almost always the first one here. That elevator had a lot to answer for.

Wanamaker was standing in front of his desk, rear-ranging papers as if they could be better sorted upside down. He was still wearing his coat, and his boots had left wet footprints on the floor.

Daisy Sue was behind her desk, her skin so pale that her make-up, usually carefully applied, almost seemed like it had been glued on.

"Do you think those detectives are any good?" she asked Eloise without saying hello. "John here thinks they should've found the killer already. What do you think?"

Eloise thought she was going to be alone in her office, that's what she thought, and she didn't want to discuss the competence or incompetence of detectives.

"I don't think it's our concern," she said, peeling off her coat. She regretted leaving her carryall here when she left for the meeting, even though she knew these two wouldn't have stolen a thing from it.

"You don't care that there's a killer at large?" Daisy Sue asked.

"Oh, I care," Eloise said, wondering if that was really true. She had assumed—and still assumed—that the killer had only targeted Dr. Carlson, but she wasn't going to say that. "I just can't do much about it."

"Even though you found the body?" Wanamaker asked, his deep voice rumbling.

No one had mentioned that at the big meeting. No one had said a word officially that she had found the body.

She almost asked how he knew that—hell, how had Micah known that too—but she didn't. She just wanted to get to her desk.

"Luck of the draw," she said. "Someone had to find him."

She had to ease past Wanamaker, who seemed uncertain about whether or not he was going to stay at his desk or leave.

"You think? I heard he'd been out there for hours," Wanamaker said.

"I don't know," Eloise said curtly. "It's not something I want to think about."

She pushed past him to her desk. Of course, the radiator was on full, and her little corner felt like a sauna.

"Anyone mind if I open a window?" she asked.

"It's cold," Daisy Sue said.

"Not over here," Eloise said.

"I don't care," Wanamaker said. He was still rearranging papers. Eloise realized he was doing it not because they were out of order but because he was nervous.

He caught her staring at him.

"You got The Dreaded Email, right?" he asked.

"We all did," Daisy Sue said. "And you guys could've warned me. I had no idea that the rules were so strict or so stupid. It's going to be hard—"

"You should have read them before you were hired." Eloise decided she didn't care if the others were too cold. She leaned over the shelf and yanked the window open six inches. The air blew in, along with some snow from the sill.

For the first time, she didn't mind the shelf over the radiator.

"It didn't matter then," Daisy Sue said. "I was happy to get a job."

"I figured it would be easy," Wanamaker said. "I do enough TV—"

"I have work," Eloise said, cutting them off. She didn't want to have The Dreaded Email discussion today of all days.

"Before you climb into your corner," Wanamaker said, "I want your opinion."

Eloise turned slowly and looked at him. He was standing in the middle of the office, his hands filled with papers.

"I'm thinking," he said slowly, "now that Dr. Carlson's

gone, that maybe I should apply elsewhere. I mean, who wants to be known as someone who is teaching at a murder campus?"

"That's what they're going to call us?" Daisy Sue asked. "A murder campus?"

Wanamaker was staring at Eloise, though, as if Daisy Sue hadn't spoken at all.

It was taking Eloise a moment to process what Wanamaker was saying. It was the opposite of what all the other assistants were saying.

She leaned against the shelf, her legs boiling from the radiator and her back starting to freeze from the open window.

"He promised you a promotion, didn't he?" she asked, and maybe she sounded accusatory. Or maybe just confused. Because she was both.

Wanamaker didn't look like someone Dr. Carlson would champion, especially since Wanamaker was teaching something about economics in the history department.

"You haven't published enough for that." Daisy Sue stood up, her voice shrill. "You have hardly written anything. You haven't done the work. I know you haven't done the work. You hardly ever do anything. You even get other people to sub for you without acknowledgement. You're a fraud, that's what you are, and I think someone should investigate your degree. I don't even think you finished it."

That was a bit of an overreaction. Eloise moved away

from the window/radiator, toward her desk, her legs a bit wobbly from the heat.

"I finished it," Wanamaker said. "I didn't have to sleep with a professor to do it, either."

"You son of bitch," Daisy Sue said and threw a stapler at him. He ducked, and the stapler hit the back of his chair, then clattered to the floor.

Eloise retreated deep into her corner, out of the line of fire.

"I did not sleep with anyone," Daisy Sue said. "People always accuse me of that because I'm *pretty*."

"That's subject to debate," Wanamaker said.

"You ass—"

"Stop!" Eloise said. She didn't want more staplers thrown or words thrown, for that matter. She normally would have emerged from her corner to talk to them, but they were both on edge, so she didn't. "This isn't helping."

"Helping what?" Daisy Sue asked in a very vicious voice. "You?"

And suddenly, Eloise recognized that voice. It was the same one that was shouting at the man in the stairwell the day before, the voice that had sent Eloise to the wrong side of building so that she would be the one to discover Dr. Carlson.

"No," Eloise said. "Us. You're mad about the twenty percent rule, aren't you?"

Her question derailed Daisy Sue. "What?"

"I heard you fighting with someone in the main stairwell. You were mad that your book only counted as twenty percent of your publications for a promotion." Eloise took one tiny step forward so she could see Daisy Sue better.

Daisy Sue looked a lot smaller than she had before. Now, her face was suffused with color, as if she had been caught doing something wrong.

"You *heard* that?" she asked.

"Heard what?" Wanamaker asked.

Eloise was going to ignore him for the moment.

"Yeah, I heard that," Eloise said, "and boy, could I identify with it. I think every assistant who has read those guidelines has gotten angry about that part. Because you know what it does?"

"What?" Daisy Sue and Wanamaker asked in unison, even though they probably didn't mean to be in complete synch.

"It keeps us here, constantly begging the committees for a promotion. For special treatment." She waved a hand at Wanamaker. "Like your TV stuff. You think that'll get you a job at another university? It won't. But if you don't publish, then you won't have anything to show for your time here, and you'll be stuck here. Dr. Carlson would have *owned* you."

She felt a little light-headed. It was all so clear now. She had always known that the rules were made so that no one could get a legitimate promotion, but she hadn't realized what else those rules did.

"And you," Eloise said to Daisy Sue, "you already have

your book, and you're about to finish another one, aren't you?"

"Who told you that?" Daisy Sue looked a little scared now.

"You did, just now," Eloise said. "I'll bet it's not going to be published by a university press either, is it?"

"No, it's not." Daisy Sue straightened. "It's out of New York, just like my last book was. I was going to tell the committee after I'd done some more TV appearances. But they would mostly be on what you people call 'right-wing media,' so I was worried that TV wouldn't count, but if it did—"

"It doesn't," Eloise said. "Lots of other professors have done TV. It doesn't count."

Wanamaker made a small sound. "But Dr. Carlson said—"

"Yes, he did, and he probably could've made it happen for you." Eloise frowned. "I'll wager the committee was starting to get some blowback."

"Blowback?" Daisy said, and then nodded. "Yes, of course. Blowback. If I'm denied because of that 20% rule, they'll get blowback from me, and I have reach. I have 10,000 followers on X, and they can be mobilized. I wonder what they'll think when they learn that it's been three years since a woman got promoted in this department."

"They'll think that's the way of things," Wanamaker said. "Know your audience. Twitter—I mean X— doesn't care what happens to women or people of color. If you were on—"

"I don't want to discuss social media," Daisy said, waving her hand dismissively, even though she was the one who had initially brought it up. "But I have to say that I can't believe that good old Dr. Carlson would want to promote someone like you."

Eloise almost closed her eyes, but if she did that, then she would miss the trainwreck unfolding in front of her.

"Someone like me?" Wanamaker said.

"Usually, the unworthy are white males," Daisy Sue said. "They cluster."

They did, although Eloise was a bit surprised that Daisy had noticed.

"Maybe he thought I was worthy of a promotion," Wanamaker said. "Maybe he was going to champion me because of my work."

"Seriously?" Daisy asked. "Your scholarship is weak, and your personal discipline does not exist."

Okay, this was going too far. The last thing Eloise wanted was her office mates to fight like this. But Eloise was deep in the room, and couldn't figure out how to leave. From where she was standing, she couldn't even see the door.

"I am very disciplined," Wanamaker snapped. "I miss my classes on occasion because of my television work. I always have someone qualified take my spot. And Dean Chizer understands. He's very interested in the documentary that

I'm a co-writer and director of. We've got a deal for five documentaries on various topics to do with shopping in America, and it looks like we'll air on either CNN or CNBC first, or maybe Netflix—"

"Liar," Daisy Sue said. "There's no proof—"

"You want to see the contracts?" Wanamaker asked. "Or talk to my lawyer? I've been working all of this for years now. That's why Dr. Carlson said he could get my TV work considered. Because it's good for the university, unlike your little lame ass and bigoted podcasts and tiny book deals. They're not important—"

"Stop!" Eloise said. "Just stop."

They completely ignored her.

"Maybe you killed him," Wanamaker said, his voice vicious. "I mean, all it took was a brick and some fury—"

"*Stop!*" Eloise shouted.

That caught their attention. They looked at her like she had grown a third head.

"This isn't helping," she said. "It's just not. I found him. Do you know what he looked like?"

They waited, almost as if they wanted to know. And she wasn't really going to tell them, because she was never going to get that image out of her head.

"He was dead. He was frozen and it was horrible, and *she didn't do it!*" Eloise actually pointed at Daisy Sue. "Because I heard her fighting with someone—"

"Dr. Dillenger," Daisy Sue said. "I saw him on the stairs."

"—not five minutes before I went down the other stairwell. There was no way she could have hit him and then made it back to fight with Dr. Dillenger—"

"There was if Dr. Carlson had died a while ago," Wanamaker said.

"And where were you all day?" Daisy Sue said. "You're never around. Were you working on your famous documentary?"

"I think that's enough." Another voice entered the conversation, and weirdly, Eloise recognized it, even though she'd only heard it twice before.

Detective Staggher sauntered into the office. He almost looked bemused. Maybe that was how his face looked in repose.

"None of you did it," he said. "For example, Professor Granada is a smart woman who wouldn't lead us to someone she killed."

Somehow that didn't sound like real praise. But Eloise would take it.

"Professor Wanamaker here was off-campus, meeting with who, now?"

Wanamaker straightened. "I'm not supposed to say because the deal is not done yet. But someone from—"

"Hulu, I think," Staggher said. "Or maybe Paramount. Or maybe that someone was just blowing smoke up your butt, son. You seem vulnerable to that."

Wanamaker's cheeks grew dark, and his eyes glittered. But he didn't say anything.

"And you, Professor Mortimer, you were the one I was

wondering about, but when Professor Granada said that you were angry at Dr. Dillenger, is it? Fighting on the stairs, which others heard as well, but you were arguing over the 20-80 split, which," Staggher said with a bit of a nod toward Daisy Sue, "you are not alone in."

"We're all angry about that," Wanamaker said in a near growl.

Eloise was startled to hear him defend Daisy Sue, especially considering how hard they had been fighting.

"Yes, and that's the point, isn't it?" Staggher said. "You're all angry about it because, as Professor Granada said, it keeps you here and working but doesn't give you any real chance to improve your lot."

"You heard that?" Eloise asked.

"I think everyone on the entire floor heard you." Staggher walked a little deeper into the room. "But that got me thinking as you all were shouting."

Eloise was starting to get cold. The air from the window had turned even frostier, or maybe the radiator had finally shut off.

Or maybe the shiver she had felt a moment before was really about his words.

"Thinking about what?" Wanamaker asked.

"I was wondering," Staggher said slowly, "if you knew someone—an assistant professor most likely—who wasn't upset by the—what do you call it? The Damned Letter?"

"The Dreaded E-mail," Daisy Sue said. "And no, everyone I know is pissed as hell."

"Yeah, me too," Wanamaker said. "All the conversations haven't been about Dr. Carlson's death but about The Dreaded Email. It's almost like he didn't matter."

"Oh, he mattered," Staggher said. "A great number of you believed he was the one behind the faculty rules and regulations.'"

"It's all of them," Daisy Sue said. "I tracked it down. That's why I was talking to Dr. Dillenger."

Yelling at him, actually, but Eloise didn't correct her. Daisy Sue could believe that was talking if she really wanted to.

"Was there someone, an assistant professor perhaps, who wasn't upset by the Damned Letter?" Staggher asked.

He was doing that on purpose to keep them focused on his words. Eloise didn't want to focus on his words. Something else was coming to mind.

"John here," Daisy Sue said. "He seemed to think TV was publishing, which it isn't."

"Mmmm," Staggher said, and the sound was dismissive. He was staring at Eloise. "Professor Granada? Do you know something?"

That fleeting thought must have skated across her face before leaving her a bit confused. She had to focus on retrieving the thought. Something from the day before—

"Anastasia Lundgren," she said before she could stop herself. Then she did stop herself and thought about it for a moment. Eloise had no reason to protect that woman.

Anastasia Lundgren had never done anything for anyone without benefitting herself first.

"What about her?" Staggher asked.

"Last year, she was angry enough for all of us. This year, I saw her just before I found him, and she was calling herself hopelessly optimistic or something, saying that the university was going to have to make changes and people shouldn't be so upset."

"Which means nothing," Daisy Sue said. "Anyone with a brain can see that the university needs to make changes."

"But they haven't for decades," Wanamaker said. "They keep recycling the same policies, and no one fights back."

But Staggher didn't appear to be listening to them. Instead, he kept his gaze on Eloise. "What was her demeanor?" he asked.

"Calm," Eloise said. "Almost…upbeat."

"As if that woman could be upbeat," Wanamaker said.

"She hated Dr. Carlson," Daisy Sue said. "She and I were talking last week. She thought she was probably going to have to self-publish her book, you know, the one on Thoreau being a fraud?"

"It's so trendy to write about Thoreau," Wanamaker said. "Especially in feminist circles. I guess his mom fed him the whole—"

"Why would Professor Lundgren write a book like that?" Staggher asked. For the first time, he looked at Daisy Sue.

Daisy Sue shrugged. "I guess she was remaking her

cabin to be like his, to see if someone could actually do all the crap Thoreau did and still have time to write. But she was getting mad that she was going to have to keep teaching. She kept applying for grant after grant, and they kept turning her down, and Dr. Carlson laughed at her, and said that if she was going to isolate herself in the woods, then she needed to isolate herself in the woods and stop bothering the rest of us."

Another shiver ran through Eloise. And, apparently, all of that was enough for Staggher.

He nodded, an almost courtly move, and said, "Thank you for your time."

Then he pivoted and walked out of the office.

No one spoke for a good minute. Then Wanamaker walked to the door and looked up and down the hallway.

When he came back, he said, "What a weird little man."

"I researched him," Daisy Sue said. "He has the highest close rate in the police department."

Eloise went to the window and closed it. The radiator had shut off for maybe the first time all morning. It was actually a little chilly near her desk, and she didn't mind.

She sat down, then put her head in her hands.

"You okay, Eloise?" Wanamaker asked.

"Long day," she said. She realized, as she was looking down, that she hadn't wanted Dr. Carlson's death to be murder, even though it obviously was. And she didn't want the murder to be solved.

She didn't want to know that one of her colleagues was

capable of bashing someone over the head with a brick, even if he was a flaming asshole.

No one deserved to die like that.

"It's barely lunch," Daisy Sue said. "We have a meeting in an hour."

"Yeah," Eloise said. "I'll be there."

Even though she didn't want to be.

That was the story of her life at this place. Being somewhere she didn't want to be, doing something she didn't want to do.

Although she wanted to write her paper. Maybe even as a book. She wanted to stretch herself and think about other things.

She wanted, deep down, to be somewhere else.

Two days later, after a lot of sleep and some soul-searching, she found herself in the dean's office. The office was spacious. Her shared office could have fit into his private space three times over.

The furniture looked like custom mahogany, but she had no idea if he had installed it all or if it had come with the position.

Dr. Chizer looked exhausted, but somehow energetic at the same time. He was in his mid-fifties, a trim man who hiked campus like it was a mountainside he needed to conquer.

Right now, it seemed he was using a lot of caffeine to conquer this mountainside. She saw a few empty Starbucks cups in his garbage can. Since janitorial came by daily, that meant he was sucking down coffee like it was a miracle drug.

She had made this appointment herself, and had been surprised that he had time with everything going on. She would have thought that the line to his spacious office on the seventh floor of the Social Sciences Building would have been long.

Instead, the only person she had seen outside of the office was his secretary, an indomitable woman who had been at the university longer than Dr. Chizer. Longer than almost anyone, really.

She made it clear, in a surprising burst of small talk, that she was not going to miss Dr. Carlson.

Eloise had started a rough count in her head of the people who had told her that in one form or another. She was beginning to think it would be easier to count the people who would actually miss Dr. Carlson, instead of the people who wouldn't.

Dr. Chizer invited Eloise to sit down, but she didn't want to stay very long. So, she stood in front of his desk, hands folded, and knew if she was a stronger woman, she would ask for a raise and a promotion right then and now.

But she wasn't stronger.

Although she did feel a bit different.

So, she went for baby steps.

She asked for two things—an office of her own because her office mates were either fighting or sleeping with each other or both—and, equally important, she asked if she could write her own syllabi for the classes she was teaching. Because, as she pointed out, she was working off syllabi as nearly as old as the faculty guidelines—which meant they were all older than she was…and they dated from the previous century.

He pivoted slightly and pulled a Starbucks cup off the bookshelf behind him. She hadn't even noticed the cup until then. He took a long drink from it, as if contemplating the problem.

"There won't be time to order new books," he said after a moment. "You'll have to use the old ones."

"I plan to," she said. "Each class will have an interim hybrid syllabus that reflects the changes brought into the field in the last forty years or so. Next semester, I'll develop extensive syllabi and put them all in for the proper academic review. I'd actually like to take some time on developing those."

She added that last bit because there was nothing the academics around here liked more than time to review.

He studied her, as if he thought she was trying to pull something over on him. And, in a way, she was. She wasn't going to tell him that she was going to add in a few ebooks and online articles, things her students could easily access and might even feel more comfortable doing so.

She thanked him, though, finding some comfort in the

small victory. She was about to take her leave when he said, "I understand you turned Anastasia Lundgren in."

"No," Eloise said, hating that she was still at the center of faculty gossip.

It should've been Anastasia Lundgren who was the center of gossip. She had clammed up with the arrest, but her boots and jeans spoke for her. They were spattered with blood, presumably from Dr. Carlson's last moments on earth.

"I didn't turn anyone in," Eloise said. "I just thought it weird that she wasn't upset by the…"

She stopped herself from nearly blurting out the words "The Dreaded Email."

"The email?" Dr. Chizer asked. "Yes, we're now aware of how you assistants feel about it. And you are right. We should change the requirements to suit the 21st century. Would you like to be on the committee to come up with new rules?"

She caught herself mid-gasp. He was asking *her* to be on a committee? She hadn't really thought that the administration noticed her much at all.

This was only her fifth interaction with the dean, and the only one she had ever initiated.

And then he offered this? He clearly hadn't thought it through.

"I've got a conflict of interest, sir," she said. "I'd be subject to those rules."

"Every professor is subject to those rules," he said.

"They're for the entire faculty. Besides, you already have your promotion."

"What?" She felt like she had entered some kind of twilight zone. "What promotion?

"No one told you?" Dr. Chizer said. "You were approved last fall to become an associate on your next contract."

Eloise felt like the ground shifted beneath her. "No one told me, sir."

He let out a small breath, almost like he was trying to calm himself.

"Damn Carlson. He was supposed to tell you."

"Dr. Carlson was supposed to talk to *me*, sir?" Eloise asked.

"It was my idea, and it was probably a bad one," Dr. Chizer said. "I thought if you two talked, you could get past his prejudice about your research."

"My research, sir?" She was beginning to sound like a stupid parrot, repeating everything, but she couldn't stop.

"Yes," Dr. Chizer said. "Something about economics being more important than political history? Our editors at the journal are excited about the concept. They heard him discuss it, and they asked him to tell you they interested."

She hadn't really finished a satisfactory outline, and they were already interested? Because Dr. Carlson had been complaining about her?

She wasn't sure how she felt about this. Giddy, maybe.

Angry, a little. Maybe even furious, a little—at a man who was now dead.

"They actually know how to market it," Dr. Chizer was saying. He leaned back and spread his hands, as if putting his words into some kind of headline. "Something like: Elmer Granada's daughter takes him on in a scholarly battle. People eat that stuff up."

"They do, sir," she said, somehow keeping her tone even, despite all of her conflicting emotions. She was adding another onto it—the fact that she hadn't come up with that marketing angle. It was a natural one, one that— he was right—would give columnists and reviewers a hook.

She cleared her throat, mostly to remind herself to remain calm as she said, "Dr. Carlson never said anything about that, sir."

"I gather that," Dr. Chizer said. Then he threaded his hands behind his head. He looked up at the ceiling, almost like he was pretending to speak to himself. "It's a good thing that Professor Lundgren got caught quickly, don't you think?"

"Sir?" Eloise was getting whiplash from the back and forth in this conversation. Now they had returned to Professor Lundgren.

Dr. Chizer rocked forward, and his gaze met hers. His expression was as serious as she had ever seen it.

"If they hadn't caught the real killer," he said, "we all

would've been under investigation for years. Given how many people loathed Dr. Carlson."

Eloise frowned at him, wondering if there was a subtext to his comment. Did he want her to admit to hating Dr. Carlson? Because she wasn't going to.

"Um," she said, "I've been in and out of universities my entire life. My father, you know."

"I know," Dr. Chizer said, with a slight smile. After all, he had just mentioned her father.

"And," she said, "I don't think the loathing of a difficult individual is unusual in any university setting. After all, it was Woodrow Wilson who said, 'University politics are so vicious precisely because the stakes are so small.'"

Then she felt a slight twinge. Maybe she shouldn't have said that. Maybe she shouldn't have called the stakes small, because they were big for her.

A promotion meant that she could actually afford things. A promotion meant she could maybe move to another school in a year or so.

And she wanted to move, sooner rather than later.

"I thought that quote came from Henry Kissinger," Dr. Chizer said.

She bit her lip. Someone like Dr. Carlson would have fought to the death over the attribution and swore that he was right, no matter what the facts were.

She had no idea if Dr. Chizer was that sort of person, and she didn't want to find out.

"Maybe it was both of them," she said. "Given its essential truth."

Dr. Chizer let out a bark of a laugh. "I think I'm going to like working with you on the committee, Professor Granada. You'll be a welcome burst of fresh air."

"I haven't agreed yet," she said. "And I'm not sure I want to, given what happened to the person I'm replacing on the committee."

His smile faded. Right away, they were back to Dr. Carlson's death.

"Well," Dr. Chizer said, "as an associate, you're going to want to serve on a few committees. That will look good for continued promotion, which, I assume, is something you want?"

Finally, a question she could answer honestly. "Yes, sir, I do."

"Okay, then," Dr. Chizer folded his hands on top of the desk. She recognized that move. Damn near every professor used it when they were going to dole out a bit of wisdom. "You need to remember this: As long as you're on campus, it won't matter what committee you serve on or which department you're in. We're in a nest of vipers, after all. We'd all turn on each other if we could."

And then he smiled at her.

"Am I right?" he asked.

She waited half a second before responding. The politics were vicious. The stakes small.

She didn't want to lose her new promotion. She also didn't want to lose the opportunity write her book.

"Yes sir," she said as confidently as she could. "You're absolutely right."

BUT WAIT, THERE'S MORE!

Want more masterful mysteries?

Go to wmgbooks.com!

Sign up for the Kristine Kathryn Rusch newsletter, and keep up with the latest news, releases and so much more— even the occasional giveaway.

To sign up go to kriswrites.com

Get the latest news and releases from all of WMG's authors and lines, including Kristine Grayson, Kris Nelscott, *Pulphouse Magazine,* and so much more…

To sign up, **go to wmgbooks.com.**

ABOUT THE AUTHOR
KRISTINE KATHRYN RUSCH

Kristine Kathryn Rusch sold more than 35 million books worldwide. She publishes bestselling science fiction and fantasy, award-winning mysteries, acclaimed mainstream fiction, controversial nonfiction, and the occasional romance.

Her novels made bestseller lists around the world and her short fiction appeared in more than twenty best-of-the-year collections. She won more than twenty-five awards for her fiction, including the Hugo, *Le Prix Imaginales*, the *Asimov's* Readers Choice award, and the *Ellery Queen Mystery Magazine* Readers Choice Award.

To find out more about her work, go to her website, kriswrites.com

facebook.com/kristinekathrynruschwriter
patreon.com/kristinekathrynrusch
bookbub.com/authors/kristine-kathryn-rusch

www.ingramcontent.com/pod-product-compliance
Lightning Source LLC
Chambersburg PA
CBHW020637130726
47898CB00016B/1036